Berkeley, California
May–November 1896

To Beth, Lynn, Mary, Mary, and Meghan.
Thank you for marching with me.
—C. R. M.

For Lesly, idea person and determined
under-the-radar rebel, with love and thanks.
—S. S.

Thanks to the archive staff of the Bancroft Library at the University of California for their assistance in examining the Keith-McHenry-Pond Family papers, and to Mary Virginia Culbertson, Bessie's niece and Charlie's daughter, who graciously told me about her family history. Writer-illustrator Teri Sloat accompanied me on a research trip to the Bancroft archives and responded to many versions of this story. My Spokane writing group—Lynn Caruso, Beth Cooley, Mary Douthitt, Mary Cronk Farrell, and Meghan Nuttall Sayres—offered detailed feedback. An early version was read at a residency of the Hamline MFAC, a vibrant community of faculty and student writers. Finally, thanks to my husband and my ninety-two-year-old mother, who never stopped believing in me, and to Conor, Megan, and my extended family, who keep listening to my stories.

Published by
PEACHTREE PUBLISHERS
1700 Chattahoochee Avenue
Atlanta, Georgia 30318-2112
www.peachtree-online.com

Text © 2011 by Claire Rudolf Murphy
Illustrations © 2011 by Stacey Schuett

First trade paperback edition published in 2017

Illustrations rendered in gouache on Fabriano Artistico watercolor paper

Printed in October 2016 by Imago in China
10 9 8 7 6 5 (hardcover)
10 9 8 7 6 5 4 3 2 1 (trade paperback)

Library of Congress Cataloging-in-Publication Data

Murphy, Claire Rudolf.
  Marching with Aunt Susan: Susan B. Anthony and the fight for women's suffrage / written by Claire Rudolf Murphy ; illustrated by Stacey Schuett.
     p. cm.
  Summary: Not allowed to go hiking with her father and brothers because she is a girl, Bessie learns about women's rights when she attends a suffrage rally led by Susan B. Anthony.
    978-1-56145-593-5 (hardcover)
    978-1-56145-979-7 (trade paperback)
  [1. Sex role—Fiction. 2. Women's rights—Fiction. 3. Women—Suffrage—Fiction. 4. Anthony, Susan B. (Susan Brownell), 1820-1906—Fiction.] I. Schuett, Stacey, ill. II. Title.
  PZ7.M9525Mar 2011
  [E]—dc22
                                        2011002703

MARCHING
WITH AUNT SUSAN

Susan B. Anthony and the Fight for Women's Suffrage

Written by Claire Rudolf Murphy

Illustrated by Stacey Schuett

PEACHTREE
ATLANTA

Papa took my brothers hiking, but not me.

"Strenuous exercise is not for girls, Bessie," he told me.

"You're not strong enough," Enie said.

"It's not ladylike," Charlie added.

"I can ride my bicycle faster than anyone on the block,"
I told my brothers. "Even you."

"Girls shouldn't ride bicycles either," Charlie said.

And they left without me.

Inside, Mama bustled around, preparing for a party.

"I'm strong enough to hike," I said. "Papa wouldn't take me along, just because I'm a girl."

"You can help me get ready for the suffrage tea," Mama said. "Aunt Mary will be arriving soon with our guest of honor, Miss Susan B. Anthony."

"Suffrage? I'm the one who's suffering." I picked up the newspaper and stared at Miss Anthony's photo. "She looks like a crabby old lady."

"A crabby old lady who has fought fifty years for women's rights," Mama said, "even when people threw garbage at her and called her names."

At the tea, everybody swarmed around Miss Anthony. They called her Aunt Susan, even though they weren't related to her.

She spoke about the long fight for equal rights. She told us that children should grow up in a world where both men and women were free.

Later, Aunt Mary introduced me to Aunt Susan.

"Why can't girls do the same things as boys?" I asked her.

She shook her head. "When I was your age, my teacher thought only boys were smart enough to learn long division."

"That's not right," I said.

"Come to the rally in San Francisco tomorrow, Bessie. Women's votes can help change the world."

Golden Gate Auditorium was so crowded
that I could barely breathe. Aunt Susan stood on a stage,
surrounded by hundreds of roses. Her voice thundered across the
hall. "The votes of all the people, including women with men, will
surely bring about the wisest and best government the world has ever seen."
    I pulled a white handkerchief out of my purse and joined the sea of flags
waving in the air.

The day after the rally, I rode my bicycle
over to my best friend Rita's house. "You should
have heard Aunt Susan speak yesterday," I told her.

"My papa says ladies shouldn't speak in public," Rita said.

"Aunt Susan says that girls are just as smart as boys. We should
get to help make decisions too."

"Papa decides everything in our family," Rita said.

"That's not right." I looked at my best friend. "Someday I want
to vote. Let's see if we can help out at suffrage headquarters."

All through the summer, Rita and I wrote letters, licked envelopes, and painted posters. As we worked, we listened to women talk.

"Men decide everything. They even decide
if we should get to vote."
"Men decide how the children are raised."
"Men decide how the household money is spent."

"I don't understand," I said to Rita. "I get to spend my allowance any way I want. And Mama makes decisions about lots of our purchases."

"Not at our house." Rita shook her head. "Papa keeps track of every penny."

The week before the election, we visited a factory in San Francisco. Rows and rows of girls sat hunched over, sewing in a dark room. Aunt Susan encouraged them to come to our suffrage parade.

Afterward, a girl walked up. "Me and my sister did some extra sewing to help the campaign." She handed Aunt Susan two dimes. "If women win the vote, will I be able to go to school?"

I couldn't imagine not learning how to read and write. I leaned against the wall and tried to catch my breath.

Back at headquarters, I asked Aunt Susan why those girls didn't go to school.

"Many parents can't make enough money to feed their families," she told me. "So the children have to work."

"Can women getting the vote change that?" I asked.

Aunt Susan nodded. "We can work to pass laws that will help adults *and* children."

I dumped out all the coins in my purse and handed them to her. "If those girls can give money, I should too."

Later I painted a picture of the factory girl on a banner for the parade. Rita printed the letters.

Sunday afternoon before the vote, Rita, Mama, and I marched along, carrying our banner. The crowd cheered as we sang new lyrics to "My Country, 'Tis of Thee."

Our country, now from thee,
Claim we our liberty,
In freedom's name.
Guarding home's altar fires,
Daughters of patriot sires,
Their zeal our own inspires,
Justice to claim.

But then men began shouting. "Women belong
in the kitchen! Girls belong at home!"

Rita's father appeared and dragged her away.
"No daughter of mine will parade in the streets!"

A boy splattered an egg down the front of my white
dress. "What do you want to be—a man?" he yelled.

I stood frozen, watching the oozing yellow
stain spread, until Mama picked up Rita's
end of the banner and we marched on.

When he heard what had happened, Papa bought me a new white dress. If only it was that easy to win the election.

Monday after school, Mama and I stood at the ferry launch and held up a new sign.

**REMEMBER YOUR DAUGHTERS—VOTE
YES on REFERENDUM #6**

I couldn't tell if I got more pats on the head or grumbles from the men walking by. But Mama said, "It only matters how they vote tomorrow."

The day after the election, my brothers raced me home from school. Charlie grabbed the newspaper off the front porch.

"Women Lose the Vote!" he shouted.

I leaned my bicycle against the house and snatched the newspaper out of his hand.

"What are you so mad about?" asked Enie.

"Someday you'll get to vote and you don't even care. Mama is as smart as Papa, and I'm as smart as you. We should get to vote too."

Mama came out and picked up my bicycle. "Aunt Susan
says that a bicycle gives a woman freedom. Teach me how
to ride, Bessie."

"It's hard to do," I said, sitting down on the steps.

"When you first tried to ride, you kept falling and scraping
your knees," she reminded me. "But you didn't give up."

Finally I showed her what to do—how to mount the bicycle,
balance, pedal, and drag her feet to stop.

When Papa arrived home, Mama was wobbling up and down the street. "I'm sorry about the election, Bessie," he said.

"Girls should be allowed to do the same things as boys, Papa."

"Why don't we go hiking this Saturday?" he asked.

"Thanks, Papa," I said, grabbing his hand. "And Sunday there's a rally for the next suffrage campaign. Come march with Mama and me."

AUTHOR'S NOTE

Ever since I learned that women first won the vote in the Western states, I have been fascinated with the seventy-two-year struggle for American women's suffrage. I realized that I had never read about women's suffrage in my college history courses, so I set out to learn all I could. I wanted to find a real girl to write about, and eventually I found the Keith-McHenry-Pond Family Papers at The Bancroft Library at the University of California, Berkeley. Inside boxes and cartons were Bessie's journals, newspaper articles about her family's hiking, and the suffrage collection of her aunt, Mary McHenry Keith. My hands shook as I read letters from my hero Susan B. Anthony to Aunt Mary.

Marching with Aunt Susan is based on actual events in the 1896 campaign. The quote from Susan B. Anthony's speech at Golden Gate Auditorium was one she often used. The version of "My Country, 'Tis of Thee" that Bessie sings in the parade was written by Elizabeth Harnett and performed at suffrage meetings around the country.

This story is my chance to march with Aunt Susan and to thank her, Bessie, Aunt Mary, and the hundreds of thousands of women who won the vote for me and for you.

BESSIE

Bessie Keith Pond was a real girl who lived in Berkeley, California, in 1896. She had two older brothers, Enie (Enoch) and Charlie. Her father Charles was a naval commander. Her mother Emma was a painter and poet, who invented the board game Constitution. Bessie grew up in a family of avid suffragists: her grandmother, mother, and especially her aunt, Mary McHenry Keith, who was a leader in both California campaigns.

Aunt Mary was the first California woman to graduate from law school and the wife of the well-known landscape painter William Keith. She became close friends with Susan B. Anthony during her 1895 and 1896 trips to California. In 1905, when Anthony returned for one last trip to California, Uncle Willie painted her portrait.

Bessie wrote poetry and taught art and music all her life. For many years, Bessie, her father, and her brothers took month-long mountain hikes and snowshoe trips in the Sierra Nevada mountains, sometimes up to 300 miles. This was so unusual that the family was often featured in the newspaper. An article in the June 24, 1927, edition of the *San Francisco Call* described Bessie as an "athletic girl with a fondness for outdoor life."

(1886–1955)

KEITH POND

CALIFORNIA SUFFRAGE CAMPAIGN

In 1895, the California legislature agreed to let men vote on an amendment to the state constitution in support of women's suffrage. That year Susan B. Anthony traveled to California to help get the referendum on the ballot and returned in May 1896 to lead the campaign for the November election.

Hundreds of suffragists across the state organized meetings in every town. Anthony spoke up to thirty times a day at picnics, schools, factories, military encampments, farmers' markets, church conventions, labor meetings, women and men's clubs, and even poolrooms. Women and girls worked at headquarters around the state, and working women stopped by after work to donate money or take home an armload of circulars to fold and address at night. Rallies and tea parties like the ones in the story took place from May through November, along with dinner parties, including one at the Keith home, which Anthony attended.

Ten days before the election, bar owners became worried that women's suffrage could mean passage of a law ending the sale of liquor. They quickly helped register thousands of men and instructed them to vote no.

The final tally was 247,454 votes: 110,355 for; 137,099 against.

The next morning Anthony said, "I don't care for myself. I am used to defeat, but these dear California women who have worked hard, how can they bear it?"

For many years, the suffrage movement languished in California and across America. In 1911, suffragists finally got a referendum back on the California ballot. Young suffragists campaigned in the newly invented automobile and used the telephone to reach voters. On October 10, 1911, fifteen years after the events depicted in this book, California became the sixth and largest state to approve women's suffrage.

Susan B. Anthony

(1820–1906)

Susan B. Anthony was raised as a Quaker with the belief that men and women are equal. But all around her she witnessed inequality. Girls who worked at her father's mill couldn't attend school because their families needed their wages. She and the other girls at her school weren't allowed to learn long division. Later when she became a teacher, she earned only one-quarter the salary of male teachers. All these experiences made her want to work for change.

When Anthony was eighteen years old, she joined the abolitionist movement after hearing Lucretia Mott speak out against slavery. In 1851, she met Elizabeth Cady Stanton and became devoted to the cause of women's suffrage. Anthony believed that if women could vote, they could help pass laws to end slavery and to improve working conditions and the lives of the poor.

For more than fifty years Susan B. Anthony led the fight for women's suffrage along with her friend Elizabeth Cady Stanton. While Stanton wrote speeches and raised a family, Anthony campaigned across the country. She first visited California in 1871 and returned several times, including eight months during the campaign depicted in this book.

Even in her later years, Anthony was described as tireless, working night and day. At a celebration of her eighty-sixth birthday at the 1906 meeting of the National American Women's Suffrage Association, Susan proclaimed her famous rallying cry, "Failure is impossible."

In 1896, one woman reporter said she didn't believe in suffrage—until she interviewed Anthony.

"I WISH I WERE SUSAN B. ANTHONY," SHE WROTE. THERE IS SOMETHING LOVEABLE IN HER FACE AND VOICE. SHE IS BEAUTIFUL IN HER PLAINNESS AND HER SMILE IS NOT TO BE FORGOTTEN."

Susan B. Anthony died in Rochester on March 13, 1906. Memorial services were held all over the country, including one in San Francisco, during which William Keith's portrait of her was unveiled.

After Anthony's death, Bessie's aunt, Mary McHenry Keith, and many other supporters around the country lobbied to make her birthday a national holiday. That never happened. But a dollar coin features her likeness.

Susan B. Anthony died before all American women won the vote in 1920, one hundred years after her birth. But her name is forever linked with the long battle for women's suffrage.

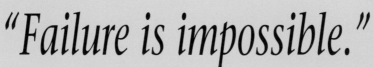

"Failure is impossible."

Suffrage History

1787	U.S. Constitution leaves voting rights up to the states to decide. Only New Jersey allows women to vote, and only between 1776 and 1807.
1866	Elizabeth Cady Stanton and Susan B. Anthony form the American Equal Rights Association, an organization for white and black women and men dedicated to the goal of universal suffrage.
1869	Wyoming Territorial legislature grants full voting rights to women.
1870	Utah Territorial legislature grants full voting rights to women.
1870	The Fifteenth Amendment allows men of color to vote, but not women.
1872	Susan B. Anthony attempts to vote in the presidential election and is arrested.
1883	Washington Territorial legislature grants full voting rights to women.
1890	Wyoming is the first state to grant full voting rights to women.
1893	Colorado state referendum grants full voting rights to women.
1896	Utah and Idaho grant full voting rights to women. Suffrage referendum defeated in California.
1906	Susan B. Anthony dies.
1910	Washington state referendum grants full voting rights to women.
1911	California state referendum grants full voting rights to women.
1912	Oregon, Kansas, and Arizona grant full voting rights to women.
1913	Alaska Territorial Legislature grants full voting rights to women.
1914	Montana and Nevada grant full voting rights to women.
1918	South Dakota and Oklahoma referenda grant full voting rights to women.
1919	U.S. House of Representatives and Senate approve the Nineteenth Amendment granting all American women full voting rights.
1920	The Nineteenth Amendment wins the necessary two-thirds ratification from state legislatures.

Our Constitution states that citizens should be allowed to vote, but it doesn't spell out who is considered to be a citizen. That was left up to each state to decide. In the early days of our country, only male landowners were allowed to vote. Men of color won the right to vote with passage of the Fifteenth Amendment in 1870, but women still could not vote.

Beginning with the first suffrage convention in Seneca Falls, New York, in 1848, women in every state worked to get the vote. The seventy-two-year campaign stretched through two wars and sixteen presidents. It included 56 state referendum campaigns, 480 campaigns to get legislatures to consider suffrage amendments, 47 campaigns for constitutional conventions, 277 campaigns directed at state party conventions, and 30 campaigns to get national parties to put suffrage in their platforms.

In 1878, the Susan B. Anthony amendment was first introduced in Congress. But it wasn't until 1919 that it finally passed both houses of Congress. In August 1920, Tennessee became the thirty-sixth state to ratify the Nineteenth Amendment. One hundred years after Susan B. Anthony's birth, women from every state finally gained the vote.

THE NINETEENTH AMENDMENT TO THE UNITED STATES CONSTITUTION

THE RIGHT OF CITIZENS OF THE UNITED STATES TO VOTE SHALL NOT BE DENIED OR ABRIDGED BY THE UNITED STATES OR BY ANY STATE ON ACCOUNT OF SEX.

CONGRESS SHALL HAVE POWER TO ENFORCE THIS ARTICLE BY APPROPRIATE LEGISLATION.

"Yes, I'll tell you what I think of bicycling. I think it has done more to emancipate women than any one thing in the world. I rejoice every time I see a woman ride by on a wheel. It gives her a feeling of freedom and self-reliance."
—Susan B. Anthony (1896)

FURTHER RESOURCES

FOR YOUNG READERS:

Failure Is Impossible: Susan B. Anthony in Her Own Words
written by Lynn Sherr (Times Books)

The History of Woman Suffrage, Volume I
edited by Susan B. Anthony and Ida Husted Harper
(General Books)

If You Lived When Women Won Their Rights
written by Anne Kamma (Scholastic)

Life and Work of Susan B. Anthony
written by Ida Husted Harper (Qontro)

*One Woman, One Vote: Rediscovering
the Woman Suffrage Movement*
edited by Marjorie Spruill Wheeler (NewSage)

*With Courage and Cloth: Winning the Fight
for a Woman's Right to Vote*
written by Ann Bausum (National Geographic)

Women of the West online exhibit:
www.theautry.org/explore/exhibits/suffrage/
suffrage_ca.html

National Women's History Museum online exhibit:
www.nwhm.org/online-exhibits/votesforwomen/
suffragetimeline.html

HerStory: www.herstoryscrapbook.com
This website features articles, letters,
and editorials regarding the suffrage campaign
from the *New York Times*

"It's up to you, Mary, and all your marvelous friends."

—Susan B. Anthony

in a letter to Bessie's aunt